ISBN 0-590-68645-3

12 11 10 9 8 7 6 5 4 3 2 1   8 9/9 0 1 2 3/0

Printed in the U.S.A.   08

First Scholastic printing, May 1998

Adapted by Molly Wigand

from the script by Jon Cooksey, Ali Marie Matheson, and Mark Palmer

Illustrated by Barry Goldberg

SCHOLASTIC INC.

New York Toronto London Auckland Sydney

The Rugrats were bored. They'd been riding in Stu's camper for hours and hours. Suddenly, bright colors flashed all around them. Pink, green, yellow, purple, red, and blue lights blinked and sparkled.

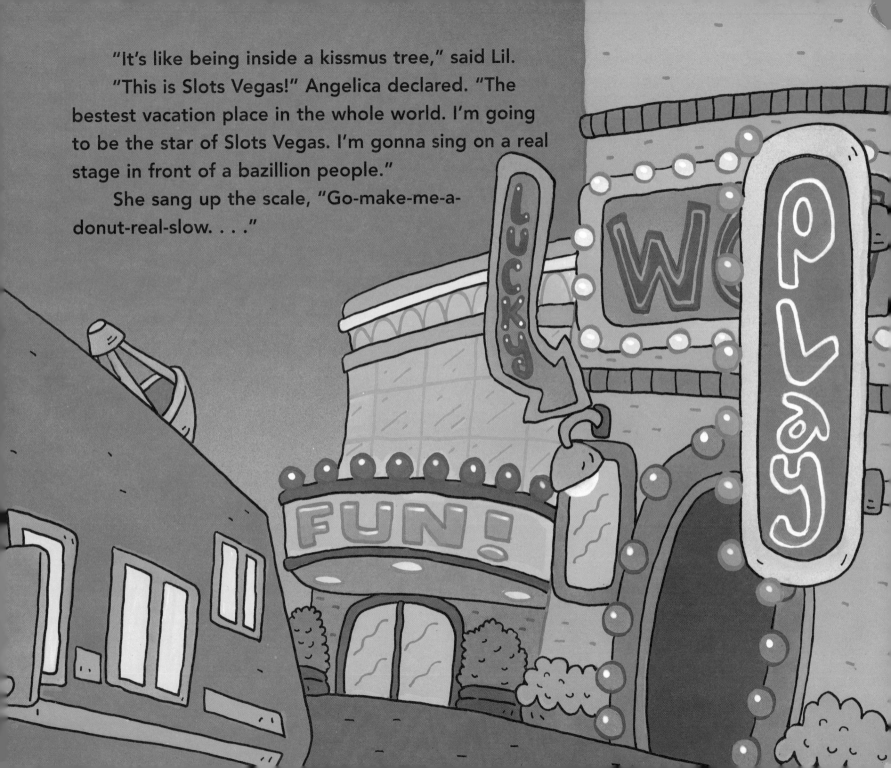

"It's like being inside a kissmus tree," said Lil.

"This is Slots Vegas!" Angelica declared. "The bestest vacation place in the whole world. I'm going to be the star of Slots Vegas. I'm gonna sing on a real stage in front of a bazillion people."

She sang up the scale, "Go-make-me-a-donut-real-slow. . . ."

On top of a fancy hotel, a huge video screen showed two men with white tigers. "There's what *I* wanna do in Slots Vegas," Tommy said.

"You wanna watch telebision?" Chuckie asked.

"No," said Tommy. "I wanna pet those kitties!"

Lil giggled. "Look at their little whispers!" she said.

"I don't know," said Chuckie. "They look kinda big to me."

The families stayed at the Viking Hotel, where a big wooden ship floated through the lobby. Strong men rowed the boat, chanting "Oh-way-oh, oh-way-oh!" They each wore a hat with two big horns.

Tommy smiled. "I think I'm going to like Slots Vegas," he said.

All the moms went out to have fun. The dads went out too—except Stu. "Looks like I'm baby-sitting," he said. Stu and the kids headed for a big buffet lunch. The table was loaded with all kinds of food. Stu wanted everything.

The babies did too! Chuckie lay under a milk machine and had milk poured right into his mouth. Phil sat in the fruit bowl. Tommy tossed in the macaroni salad. Angelica found the cake table and ate dessert after dessert. Then she noticed that a lot of people were watching her. She picked up a chocolate-covered banana.

"Good evening, lazies and dinnermen!" Angelica said loudly into her banana microphone. "Welcome to the Angelica Show, starring Angelica!"

She started singing, "Angelica the beautiful."

"Oh, beautiful, her spaceship eyes . . ."

Stu was horrified. He ran to get Angelica.

"Angelica, Angelica . . ." she screeched off-key.

Tommy looked out a window. "The kitties!" he said, pointing to the video screen at the top of a hotel. The screen showed the tigers in a cage. "It looks like they're in prism!"

"We gots to let them out, Tommy!" said Lil.

"Yeah, those kitties deserve a bacation too," Tommy said. "Come on!"

"I don't know," said Chuckie. "Maybe we should do somethin' else, like . . . sit on the floor and be really quiet."

But he went along with the other Rugrats anyway.

The babies crawled through the hotel lobby.

"Look!" said Tommy. "That big boat will take us to the kitties!" He led his friends onto the deck of the Viking ship.

Tommy, Phil, and Lil jumped up and down on a big drum. The rowers moved their oars to the drumbeat. They made the boat move fast!

Suddenly they all heard Chuckie scream, "Aaaahhhhh!" Chuckie was twirling around on a rope way up high! Then he crashed right on top of Tommy. "That's not the bestest thing to do right after lunch," said Chuckie, rubbing his tummy.

Stu heard Chuckie's scream. He grabbed Angelica and ran toward the ship. They hopped into a tiny rowboat, but it sank. Stu and Angelica had to swim to the ship!

When the babies crawled off the boat, they couldn't believe their eyes
and ears. Bright lights twinkled all around. People screamed. Bells rang.
"It's a 'musement park!" Tommy said.

Chuckie climbed onto a big green table. He tried to keep his balance as he spun around on a red-and-black twirling wheel.

"Hang on, Chuckie," said Tommy, "I'm comin'!" He pushed over hundreds of colorful chips as he rescued Chuckie from the roulette wheel.

Then Tommy and Chuckie spotted Grandpa Lou. Grandpa put a nickel in a slot machine. Tommy climbed up Grandpa's machine and stood on the handle. Suddenly the handle slipped forward. The pictures on the machine spun around, and bells started to ring. Nickels gushed out, spilling all over the floor!

"Ooo-hoo, jackpot!" cried Grandpa Lou.

The Rugrats were having fun! In a hallway that was covered with snow, they found dogsleds with fluffy brown dogs. The babies climbed into a sled.

Phil pulled an orange out of his diaper. "I saved this from lunch," he said, throwing the fruit in front of the dogs. They dashed after it.

"Aaaaaaaaaaaahhhhhhhh!" cried the babies.

The babies' dogsled was fast! The dogs ran past two skiers—Chuckie's and the twins' dads!

"Whee!" the babies cheered.

The sled sped through the snow and into . . .

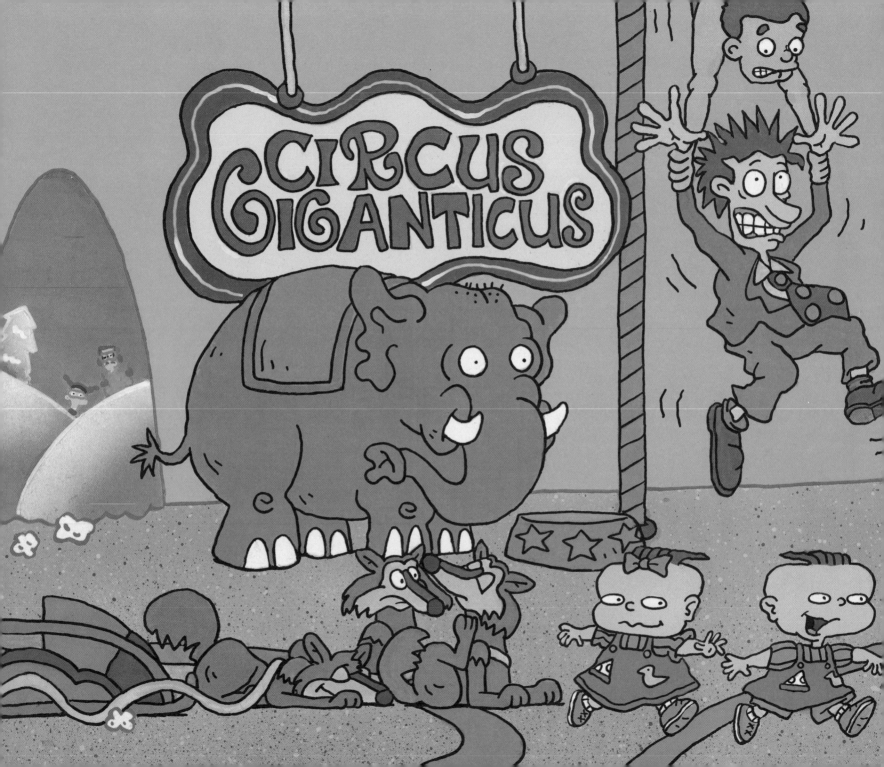

a busy circus ring!

"Clowns," Chuckie said, as bright red-and-white faces surrounded him. "It had to be clowns."

"I'll bet we're almost to the kitties," said Tommy. "Let's go!"

Stu and Angelica were on another sled right behind the babies.

"I'm coming, kids!" Stu yelled. He got off the sled and started running, with his arms outstretched, toward the center ring. A trapeze artist suddenly swung down and grabbed Stu's arms.

"What are you doing?" Stu screamed as he flew through the air.

"Aren't you part of this act?" the trapeze man asked.

"Noooooooooooooo . . ."

On her own again, Angelica found an empty clown car.

"Like my new car?" she asked the babies. "I'm going somewhere to sing and be famous."

Tommy pointed at the big video screen. "If you take us there, you can be on TV."

Angelica smiled. "Hop in, babies," she said. Then she called to Stu as they drove away. "See ya later, Uncle Stu. We're going to see the kitties!"

The clown car putt-putted out the door! People tried to get out of its way. One of the people looked very familiar.

"Uh-oh, it's my daddy!" cried Angelica, just before crashing into him.

Then she sped away.

Grandpa and Stu caught up with Drew.

"Angelica said something about the kitties," Stu said.

Spotting a poster of the tigers and their trainers, Drew blurted, "You don't think she meant—"

"They're trying to see the tigers in the Heimlich and Bob Show!" Stu yelled. The three men ran over to the show's entrance. A mean usher stopped them.

"You can't get in without tickets!" he said.

Inside the theater, a voice boomed. "Good evening, and welcome to the Heimlich und Bob Show! Tonight we will perform our famous Disappearing Act. We will lower ourselves into the cage of tigers. We will become invisible. Und finally we will reappear in this vat of lowfat milk!"

The babies watched from high above the stage. Chuckie's knees shook.

"Tommy, those kitties are gigantic!" he whispered.

Then one of the tigers looked up at Tommy with sad kitty-cat eyes.

Tommy stamped his foot. "I don't care how big the kitties are. We gotta get 'em out of that prism!"

As the babies watched, five men loaded animals into big wooden boxes. When the workers weren't watching, Angelica jumped into a box with some rabbits. Then one of the men pushed Angelica's box onto the stage.

The workers placed animals in four other boxes. Each baby jumped into a box. Soon all five boxes were on the stage.

"These boxes are completely empty," Heimlich said. "But now we close the boxes und tap on them three times, und behold . . ."

Angelica popped out of a box—along with some rabbits! "It's the fabulous ME!" Angelica sang, as the other babies jumped out too.

Back at the hotel, Didi, Betty, and Charlotte happened to glance up at the big video screen.

"Oh, my gosh!" cried Betty. "It's the babies!"

"With the tigers!" yelled Didi.

The moms dashed across the street to save their children.

Hurrying past the usher, Charlotte yelled, "Get out of my way!" The other moms ran right behind her. On the stage, Tommy had just unlocked the tiger's cage when Didi came swinging on a vine toward him. She swooped down to grab her baby.

Finally able to get into the theater, Grandpa Lou ran toward the stage and threw his bags of nickels down. The bags burst open, spilling silvery coins everywhere!

Just then, the tigers got out of their cages! Heimlich and Bob slipped on the nickels. *Splash!* They tumbled into the milk, and it spilled onto the stage.

The tigers tasted the milk at their feet. It was so good, it made them purr. Chuckie, Tommy, Phil, and Lil petted the tigers. Their moms and dads watched and smiled.

"This is the bestest bacation any baby ever had," Tommy said.

"Yeah," said Chuckie. "Except for the clowns."